HELLO NEIGHBOR

HAITI

by Jeri Cipriano

LOOK! BOOKS™

Red Chair Press   Egremont, Massachusetts

Look! Books are produced and published by Red Chair Press:

Red Chair Press LLC   PO Box 333   South Egremont, MA 01258-0333

www.redchairpress.com

Publisher's Cataloging-In-Publication Data

Names: Cipriano, Jeri S.

Title: Haiti / by Jeri Cipriano.

Description: Egremont, Massachusetts : Red Chair Press, [2019] | Series: Look! books : Hello neighbor | Interest age level: 004-008. | Includes index, Now You Know fact boxes, a glossary and resources for further reading. | Summary: "Like any neighbor, Haiti and the United States share many things in common and things that are different. In this book, readers will discover how children's lives in Haiti are similar to their own, and how they differ."--Provided by publisher.

Identifiers: ISBN 9781634403290 (library hardcover) | ISBN 9781634403719 (paperback) | ISBN 9781634403344 (ebook)

Subjects: LCSH: Haiti--Social life and customs--Juvenile literature. | Haiti--Description and travel--Juvenile literature. | United States--Social life and customs--Juvenile literature. | United States--Description and travel--Juvenile literature. | CYAC: Haiti--Social life and customs. | Haiti--Description and travel. | United States--Social life and customs. | United States--Description and travel.

Classification: LCC F1915.2 .C56 2019 (print) | LCC F1915.2 (ebook) | DDC 972.94 [E]--dc23

LCCN: 2017963407

Photo credits: iStock except for the following; p. 3, 14: blickwinkel/Alamy; p. 6: Library of Congress; p. 7: imageBROKER/Alamy; p. 11: Dreamstime; p. 13: Melvyn Longhurst/Alamy; p. 17: Eye Ubiquitous/Alamy; p. 19: Getty Images

Printed in the United States of America

0918 1P CGS19

Table of Contents

All About Haiti

Bonjou! Ou byen? Hello from Haiti [HAY-tee]. Haiti is a country in the Caribbean (kuh-RIB-ee-uhn) Sea. Haiti shares an **island** with the Dominican Republic. The island is called Hispaniola.

By airplane, Haiti is two hours from Florida. Haiti and the United States are neighbors.

FLORIDA U.S.A.

4

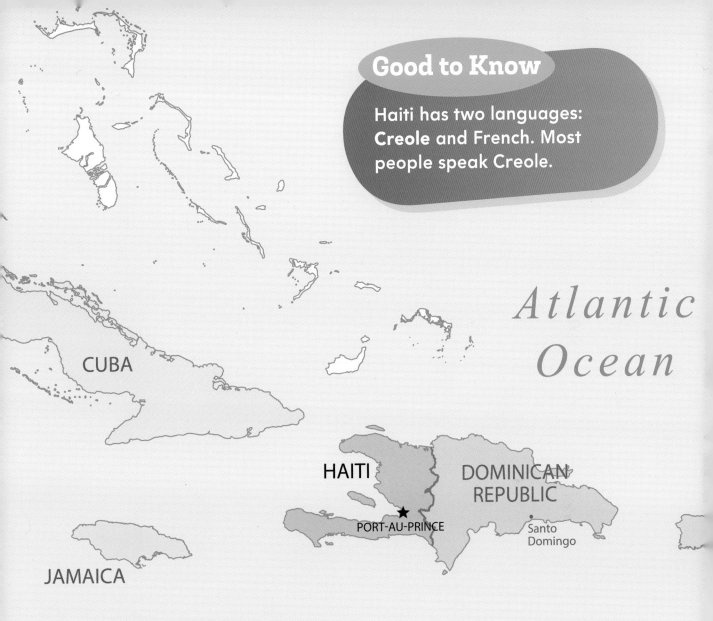

Atlantic Ocean

CUBA

HAITI

DOMINICAN REPUBLIC

★ Santo Domingo

PORT-AU-PRINCE

JAMAICA

Carribbean Sea

The name for Haitian money is *Gourde* (rhymes with "mood").

Money Talks

The man on the front of the bill is a great hero. His name was Toussaint L'Ouverture. He helped Haiti win its **independence** from France in 1804.

Good to Know

Who is on the front of the 1 dollar bill in the United States? He is a great American hero.

The flag of Haiti is blue and red. In the center is Haiti's **coat-of-arms**.

The country's **motto** is written in French. It means: "Unity (YOO-nuh-tee) Makes Strength."

The **capital** of Haiti is Port-au-Prince. Here, Haiti's president lives in a big white house called the National Palace. The palace was destroyed in a huge earthquake in 2010. It is being rebuilt now.

Good to Know

Do you know this house? It is where U.S. presidents live in Washington, D.C.

A Special Place

Haiti has a Taíno Museum. It honors the native people who were the first settlers of Haiti.

Good to Know

Taíno people passed around a "talking stick" to give everyone a chance to speak. Whoever held the stick could talk without interruption.

Many Taíno families would live in each round hut.

The Land

Hayti is the Taíno name for the country. It means "land of the mountains." Haiti has the most mountains of any Caribbean country.

Haiti has a tropical climate. The weather is hot year-round. People wear loose colorful clothes.

Good to Know

The highest mountaintop is almost two miles high!

The People

Haitian people are a mix of cultures: African, French, Spanish, and native Taíno. They love bright colors and lively music.

Children wear bright colors. They dress alike when they go to school.

Celebrations

January 1: Independence Day

On this day in 1804, black slaves won their freedom from the French.

Haitians eat soup on Independence Day. Why soup? Under French rule, there was a law that only the upper class could eat soup. Cooking and eating soup is how Haitians celebrate "being free."

Good to Know

Haiti was the first free black nation in the world.

January 2: Ancestor's Day

On this day, Haitians remember those from the past who fought for independence. They dance in the streets.

Carnival

The biggest celebration of the year is Carnival, which is usually in February. People wear fancy clothes. They march in parades and dance in the streets.

21

Words to Keep

capital: city where a nation's government is based

coat of arms: the special sign of a nation

Creole: a language and culture of French and African mix

Independence: being free from control of others

Island: land surrounded by water

motto: a saying that stands for a country

tropical: having warm and humid weather

Learn More at the Library

Books (Check out these books to learn more.)

Bartell, Jim. *Haiti* (Exploring Countries). Blastoff Readers, Bellwether Media, 2011.

Raum, Elizabeth. *Haiti* (Countries Around the World). Heinemann, 2011.

Web Sites (Ask an adult to show you this web site.)

Taíno Museum in Haiti   http://tainomuseum.org

Index

About the Author

Jeri Cipriano has written and
edited many books for young readers.
She likes making new friends
from different places. Jeri lives
and writes in New York state.